AMERICA IS PARADISE

Dr. François Adja Assemien

America is Paradise by Dr. François Adja Assemien

This book is written to provide information and motivation to readers. Its purpose is not to render any type of psychological, legal, or professional advice of any kind. The content is the sole opinion and expression of the author, and not necessarily that of the publisher.

Printed in the United States of America.

FROM THE SAME AUTHOR

* The Golden Rules for Personal Success, Health, Happiness and Salvation, Handbook, Edilivre, 2016

* Introduction to philocure, essay, Edilivre, 2016

* The African Rebels, novel, Page Turner, 2o2o

* Forbidden Africa, novel, Edilivre, 2016

* The way to live in America, guide, Edilivre, 2019

* The Current slavery in Africa, essay, Global Summit House, 2020

* The World is worth nothing, essay, Edilivre, 2016

* Côte d'Ivoire hurts, essay, Edilivre, 2018

* African Consciousness, essay, Edilivre, 2016
* Moral and spiritual education, essay, Edilivre, 2016
* Président Donald Trump et les Africains, essai, Edilivre, 2020
* Thomas Sankara comme Thomas More et Socrate, essay, Ouagadougou, 2020
* Ahikaba, novel, Mary Bro Foundation Publishing, London, 2018
* Electoral code, novel, EBAV Stars, 1995
* Portrait of good and bad voter, of good and bad candidate, essay, Black Stars, 2000
* Côte d'Ivoire with its foreigners, essay, Black Stars Editions, 2002
* Political thought to save Côte d'Ivoire, essay, Afro Star, 2003
* Let's save humanity and life, essay, Global Summit House, 2021
* Corona virus, essay, Global Summit House, 2020.

I DEDICATE THIS BOOK

To

Thomas Hung Phan
(for his humanism and generosity)

Margarita Begazo
(for her humanism and generosity)

CONTENTS

INTRODUCTION

We want to present here a phenomenon that we call **American moral humanism.** The United States of America is a country which practices a very bold moral humanism. That deserves to be taught to the world. It is observable in the daily live of Americans. This can be observed through the institutions and the functioning of all the states that make up the American federation. What is humanism? What is morals? How do these two things manifest in the life of Americans? By humanism, we mean the policy of a country that promotes progress, development and happiness of human beings or of its population. Humanism is the national policy which respects dignity and all basic human rights. Humanism thus represents the promotion or the legitimate valorization of superior human qualities and ascetic moral virtues.

When man fights to know, improve and defend what constitutes the true humanity, he is doing moral humanism (know yourself Socrates said). It is about the embellishment, the preservation, the enrichment, the development of the intrinsic values of the man. Moral humanism is simply the defense of the higher interests and the fundamental rights of men forming a people, a community, a society. Moral humanism thus understood is opposed to naturalism, that is to say the study or knowledge of nature. Humanism has given rise to the so-called human or social sciences: psychology, sociology, anthropology, morals, ethics, historiography, law, economics, linguistics, philosophy, literature. Naturalism constitutes the set of so-called exact and experimental sciences: chemistry, biology, physics, astronomy, ecology...

The American humanism merges morality. Indeed, what is morality of a people? It is the course of action or a system of rules chosen by a society. It is the compass of this society. It is its scale of values, which guides, orients all its practices, all its behaviors, all interpersonal relationships. It determines all its actions, defines good and bad. Morality of a people represents his thought or his vision of good and evil which illuminates and envelops his habits and customs. The customs of a people are inspired and determined by his thinking of good and bad (his morality). The idea of the good of a society is the nucleus or the central pillar of its customs, of its habits. Morals aims for the good and the happiness of men. It fights, condemns, forbids evil, synonymous with misfortune. It shows what is good, fair, useful. Morals translates into judgments which state the good, the permissible values. It comes from Reason, from consciousness. It is the collective rule or norm, the general will, the popular consensus. Morals defends the general interest, the common good or the happiness of all. The end of human life is happiness and therefore good. The idea of good is absolutely present in the ideal of happiness. These two things are inseparable, consubstantial. Human beings are in constant search of happiness. They want to be happy. But they must go through the good, that is to say the good act, the virtuous actions to be hqppy. This is the sine qua non condition for achieving happiness. The practice of ascetic virtue (good) gives happiness. So no one has an interest in harming his neighbor. No one is wicked willfully, consciously, according to Socrates. Wickedness is the effect of ignorance. It is a mistake about the nature of the good. The villain is mistaken about the nature of the good he wants to do because he can only want good (and never bad) for everyone and for himself. For he seeks happiness which is dependent on good. Every wicked person is therefore ignorant. Socrates, the first Greek humanist of Antiquity, thus strongly underlines the capital importance of moral knowledge. Besides, he reduces all knowledge to morals as a fundamental and salutary science. For him, the good and the true are identical, inseparable. This is verifiable in America. We will try to prove this assertion by studying the condition of life of the different categories of beings living in America: woman, child, old man, animal, plant.

THE CONDITION OF WOMEN

Moral humanism regulates and protects the life of women in America. Women are queens in America. Every woman is a queen in the USA. America gives a special status to women. Indeed, women are perceived as superior, sacred beings. So they deserve special and absolute respect. No man has the right to offend them, to abuse them, to oppress them, to mistreat them. They enjoy the full protection of state laws. Their security, development and defense are perfectly and effectively guaranteed by an educational, legal and police system. Their adversaries are men. They are in positive rivalry and in constant fair competition with men (sexism). It is present in the detail of life and even in their marital home. They are brought up and educated with the spirit not to cede supremacy, authority to men but to share all powers and rights with them. They are formed to be independent of men, free, sovereign and equal to them on all possible levels. They must not suffer any discrimination linked to their nature as women. They must not be despised, humiliated, degraded, dominated, underestimated, belittled by men (phallocratic danger). Women have the same rights as men with regard to education and employment as well as in all areas of human and societal activity. Nothing and absolutely nothing is forbidden or refused to them because of their sex. They are entitled to everything they can deserve through their efforts, intelligence, work, socio-professional training, courage and endurance.

Their merit, competence and talents make their rights and value in the same way as in men. Women and men are appreciated, judged in the same way, according to the objective criteria required by the various social, professional, administrative, economic, technical, scientific and political activities. Women are not the slaves or the subordinate of men. They do not play the supporting roles as it is seen elsewhere, in other countries, in particular in Africa and in the East. They are not victim of injustice, arbitrariness, inequality, violence or unfavorable prejudices. On the contrary, they rightfully enjoy a positive and glorious image. They are highly valued. They are put in the place of honor. They were given all the chances, all the possibilities of their total success and maximum development. Thus women were able to tread the lunar soil just like men, their rival, did. They are in a relationship of equality, justice, mutual respect with men. They are emancipated, free and worthy. They are fulfilled. They are not marginalized but rather present in normal, official, American life.

In truth, women have more rights than men. They are naturally listened to and more considered than men. Justice is legitimately and morally in their favor. If a woman is married and has to get a divorce, she enjoys a lot of benefits. For example, justice gives her most of the time the family home as her personal property. Her spouse is evicted from this house. He is dispossessed of it. He must also financially assist his spouse after the divorce until their children (if they have any) are of age (child support). He owes damages to his wife, if he is wrong, on pain of being imprisoned or constrained by law as the case may be, the need, the necessity. If he rapes his wife, he is imprisoned. To rape one's wife is to make genital love to her without her consent, despite her refusal, against her will. It is brutalizing her, sexually assaulting her. It's having sex with her when she doesn't want to or when she is either tired or angry. Some women in bad faith slander their husbands to the police by accusing them of rape. And domestic violence is very severely punished. The man who beats his wife is punished. He is considered as a criminal. There also, women who are dishonest unjustly imprison their innocent husbands whom they want to get rid of by slandering them to the police.

Married women are granted the right to own and manage their income, property in their own name if their spouses are unable to do so. Women have the right to vote and to be elected at all political levels. Currently Ms. Kamala Harris is the Vice President of the United States of America. The President is Mr. Joe Biden.

2

THE CHILDREN CONDITION

What is the condition of children in America? What do children receive from society? How are children treated? Children are kings in America. They are highly respected, loved, protected, nurtured and defended by society. They are very spoiled. They must not be subjected to any form of violence or mistreatment. A father (or mother) who beats his child is punished. He goes to jail and his child is taken away from him. From birth, the American child begins to benefit from free services and care of all kinds of the government. He is supported on all fronts. His school education, health care, physical and moral security, food, clothing etc. are insured and guaranteed. He benefits from health insurance, school scholarship, food stamp. At school, he receives free school supplies and eats for free. He is transported free of charge by the school buses. The federal government and the local government jointly manage his life in a human and healthy way. His family spends very little money on his life.

The various charitable institutions and associations existing in America also provide very valuable help or support to parents. They take good care of the children in terms of education, health, food, clothing etc. Children are the most precious human asset. They belong to the state and to all of society. Everyone owes him tenderness, affection, love, sympathy, kindness, generosity, assistance. Everyone works for their best growth, happiness, well-being and success. Everyone is fighting for their harmonious, happy and fruitful integration into society. Indeed, every-one is aware that children are the future of the world. It is an important investment for the progress, prosperity and future of society. It is the children who will make the success, hap-piness, greatness and power of the country. It is truly the fundamental and most profitable investment in the world. The Americans have understood this well. So they really take great care of children. They do not skimp on the means necessary to make their young people a very competitive force. They want bright, happy, responsible and worthy young people. So America spends an enormous amount of money, energy and intelligence to perfect the training and education of its young people in all fields of activity. America has understood this better than the rest of the world. That's why it has a lot of champions and a lot of geniuses. Thus it dominates the whole world on all levels. It tirelessly cultivates the spirit of excellence. It instills this in its population and its young people. Thus very early on, the American children performed feats in school and in life. They are put in fierce competi-tion. They are everywhere and always in competition. They are educated and trained as warriors to be always and everywhere the best and champions of the world. America needs only the braves, the geniuses and the heroes. Each child is required to do everything to become the best possible citizen and servant of his country. He intended his life for the glory, the greatness, the success, the happiness, the honor, the power, the prosperity and the infinite prestige of his country (Olympic Games). America the best. America the beautiful. America first. America the greatest. This is the mindset of American children. They are very fervent winners, nationalists and patriots.

3

THE CONDITION OF OLD PEOPLE

Old people are the senior citizens. They benefit from special care and advantages. They are exceptionally respected and maintained. Generally, they have made a success of their life. They are either in their own houses or in cities built for the elderly. So Leasure World in Maryland. These cities are equipped with all the institutions and all the vital cultural, sporting, social and economic infrastructures: hospitals, banks, firefighters, post offices, restaurants, churches, sports grounds, swimming pools, supermarkets, public gardens, training rooms, gymnastics, computers, shows, libraries etc.

The elderly benefit from retirement pensions, charities and health insurance which watches over them and manages their health (social security). Their safety, health, well-being, peace, tranquility and happiness are guaranteed until their death. They receive special and total attention from the federal and local governments. They are in the spotlight. All their basic needs are met diligently. They are not in need or in precariousness. They are very worthy and very happy.

Elsewhere, especially in neocolonized Africa, old people are forgotten, neglected, condemned to misery, suffering and death. They are pitiful. There is no official or private social service to help them live. They thus left the world and life before their often precipitous death. Nothing is done to make them happy or to safeguard their dignity. They are despised, mocked, humiliated. Old age is an ordeal, an unbearable decline, a great misfortune. It is saddening and shameful. Governments do not maintain the elderly properly, honorably, humanely. Thus the old people confine themselves to their villages to await the death almost desired by some. Better to die than to suffer. This is the philosophy of some old people. They die early under the weight of worries, poverty, misery, suffering, decay. Everything shows old people that they are useless, unwanted and unworthy of continuing to live.

There is no policy put in place by governments to help old people live well, be safe, healthy, at peace, happy, worthy. So old people are like beggars. They are like outcasts, ostracized. Africans will benefit from imitating the American policy of managing the elderly. So the world will be fairer and life will be more beautiful in Africa. For all men are called to become old men. It is inevitable. No one will escape it. Each of us will be old if he is lucky enough to live long. To be an old man is a natural, common, universal fate. It is a law of nature, a necessity. Unless you die young. It is the only way to escape from being an old man. It is the duty of society as a whole to maintain and support the elderly until their beautiful natural death. Each old man must be able to enjoy respect for his person and for the dignity of the human person which is inherent in him.

4

THE CONDITION OF ANIMALS

Animals are treated very well like humans in America. They are very well protected and defended by morals and law. They are not neglected, assaulted, mistreated or massacred by men as is done elsewhere, in other countries, especially in Africa. They have the right to life, health, security, well-being, respect, happiness, peace and tranquility. In short, they have all the basic, vital rights that humans enjoy. Pets are medically monitored.

Dogs and cats, for example, have health insurance. They are very well looked after by vets in the event of illness. Their owners must be human, loving, compassionate, charitable, kind, worthy and very responsible to them. They have a duty and an obligation to love, feed and maintain their animals properly. If they fail in this duty, they are severely punished by justice. There are associations of animal friends and advocates. They control animal owners, hold them to account and watch over the fate and rights of animals.

Wild animals enjoy the same care and benevolence. No one has the right to attack, kill and eat them as is done freely in Africa. Deers, rabbits, snakes, squirrels, ducks, foxes etc. are perfectly safe. They live in harmony, in peace, with men without any fear, without any danger. They roam freely everywhere as do dogs, sheep in African villages. They enter yards, garages and private gardens without being in any danger. If you kill one on purpose, you'll go straight to jail. Your neighbors and cameras will report you to the police. Rather, you have to protect them. Animals are kings, free and rulers in America. It is the opposite elsewhere, in particular in Africa, where animals are without any rights, where the wild animals are exterminated at leisure. There is no law for the safety and protection of animals in Africa. Besides, no law is respected by anyone in Africa. The beasts are considered mortal enemies of men. The animals are without interest, without value in the eyes of Africans. They are only food (meat). We must kill them wherever we find them. We must not spare the life of a snake, a lion, a tiger, a panther, a leopard, a cheetah, a rat, a bird, an elephant, a doe, a gazelle, a caiman, a fish. Never. They are sworn and deadly enemies. They are barely good to eat or sell. So they are being decimated in Africa. Hunters or poachers massacre them with joy and with impunity. The African government classified forests and bushes that lock up all rare animal species. But those places are gruesome battlefields and wars. This is where the world's greatest hunters exercise their talents and their cruel killer professions. Poor helpless beasts! Wickedness against animals is a popular festival in Africa. This brings the greatest joy to the ruthless Africans.

5

CHARITY AND ALTRUISM

The American people are very charitable and very selfless. They like to give, to offer money, furniture, clothes, shoes, food etc. to strangers, to the needy. It is their pleasure (good will). This act is called donation. It is taught to children at school and in families. Parents willingly donate money to their children to donate to school. A multitude of institutions, associations and non-governmental organizations practice charity towards the poor, the needy and foreigners (CASA of Maryland, churches, temples, mosques, departments of health and social services etc.). The federal government and all the states also give charity. They offer food (food stamp), housing or pay rent to the needy (homeless, unemployed, refugees...). They pay bills for water, electricity, gas, medical care for the poor. They give them health insurance. They offer scholarships to learners (free school supplies).

All social and human problems have their solutions in America. There are helpers all over the place. You just have to expose your problem, whatever it is, on social networks, inform those around you, make announcements and you receive help from others. Just be informed in order to benefit from the works of charity, altruism and humanism that exist everywhere. Thanks to charity, people in America do not suffer to much from the present global health crisis (covid-19). In fact, the federal government and other governments are offering money to people. It is a very good support that saves human lives (stimulus checks).

In this very cruel time of covid-19, solidarity, charity, compassion, generosity, altruism, empathy, humanism and patriotism are eagerly awaited and very welcome from peoples and Presidents. All nations must fully manifest these values for the happiness and salvation of mankind. Everything must be done to shame and defeat the creators, promoters and profiteers of corona virus around the world. They are Free masons, Illuminati, mystics, corrupt politicians, Satanists, religious, eugenic philosophers and globalists. They are the worst enemies of mankind. They are still on the offensive to create what they call the new world order by force. They want to wipe out humanity and replace it with zombies and robots thanks to the feats, the prodigious progress of science and technology. Their weapons are Bible, covid-19, vaccines, gene therapy, 5 G, spreading, corruption, cunning, demagoguery, lies, Machiavellianism, fear. They are both wolves and foxes, saints and devils, angels and demons, good and evil, heaven and hell. They are very powerful deceivers and manipulators present everywhere on earth. Their intermediaries and accomplices are the Presidents, the business-men and the intellectual elites. So they rule earth and want to kill over 90% of the world's population. They are organized into a terrorist and predatory mafia. They want to create a collectivist world government, a digital world currency, a world army (NATO) to control, subdue, alienate all humans. They are pure wizards, vampirs, leviathans. The world is in danger! Life is in danger! Humanity is in danger! We are in the real first world war now. Run for your life. Fear has made everyone a slave. Ignorance has turned people into sheep and prisoners. So humanity accepts everything: confinement, wearing face masks, vaccines, unemployment, poverty, misery and death. Time is too serious. Humanity must wake up, stand up and break free. It must conquer, recover all its fundamental rights which are currently stolen from it, torn away by cunning, barbarism, force, cynicism, lies, dishonesty and fear. Fear always makes slaves and the cowardice of these slaves keeps them in mortal bondage.

6

HOSPITALITY

America is very hospitable. Its history is dominated by hospitality. Its life is based on hospitality. Its inhabitants and its rulers are very welcoming. This is how it was created and rapidly developed to become the greatest country in the world. Its hospitality consists in opening all its doors and all its borders to the whole world. It is the crossroad of earth. It welcomes men and women from everywhere. It is home to all races, cultures of the world and all of humanity. Its population is biologically and culturally mixed. There are Indians, natives, Europeans, Africans, Asians, Oceanians and others. America is built by all the peoples of earth. And that makes its strength, its greatness, its prosperity, its wealth, its power and its originality. This explains its all-out dominance over the world. Indeed, America is made up of the dynamic gathering of all the peoples of earth with their civilizations, their knowledge, their know-how. It is an integrated and integrative society.

In this historical and sociological dynamic, America welcomes new immigrants day by day. It remains true to itself, to its history, to its tradition and to its culture. Such is its destiny. America is the land of migrants. Thus it cannot refuse hospitality to people who come to enrich it, to develop it further. So true is it that unity is strength, prosperity, success, security, and salvation. America has understood very well and learned very well the lesson of the migratory and hospital dynamics. It derives a lot of benefits, pleasure and happiness from that. America is the biggest profiteer of this law more than any other country in the world. Hospitality is its golden rule, its reason for living and its reason for being. It is its quid proprium, its substance, its essence, its ipseity. It is his destiny.

In truth, all the great countries in the world are created by foreigners. All owe their success, their development, their prosperity, their happiness, their power and their salvation to strangers. They owe that to the creative genius of peoples from elsewhere. This is where the value of migrants lies. America would not have existed without the arrival of the English on the land which became America by their fact. The Indians (natives, aborigines) did not create the United States of America. This is the fate of all the colonies in the world. America and Canada are the work of English settlers. Quebec is the work of French colonists. Mexico is the work of the Spanish colonists. African countries are the work of European settlers. In Asia, the same European settlers worked and built powers. Foreigners are indisputable builders of country, creators of history and civilizations. So a country which refuses foreigners at home condemns itself and refuses its happiness, its development, its greatness, its power and its salvation. It thus rejects its glory. France is currently the world soccer champion thanks to its foreigners, its Black and African immigrants. Most of the world champions in sport and super stars in art in every western country are of foreign origin. In this way, a host of artists, athletes, inventors, scientists, thinkers, and foreign workers make honor, pride, prosperity, success and glory of America and of European countries. Foreigners are then adorable. They are very valuable. They are geniuses, heroes, saviors. Xenophobia must therefore disappear from this world. It doesn't make sense. Africans must understand this and imitate the American example. America's power is due to the fact that it was able to create the union of 50 states (federation). All federations are strong, powerful, prosperous, rich and happy. They dominate, control the small states. African micro-states will find their salvation in uniting, in federating to create together their liberating power. The path to African renaissance necessarily passes through this. Union, discipline, hospitality and hard work make a beautiful country. That makes great countries. It is a lesson for Africa.

7

HONESTY

Honesty is a cardinal American virtue. Americans are honest. It's undeniable. It has allowed them to build the most beautiful nation and the greatest power in the world for themselves. They are not cheaters, liars, thieves, thugs, corrupters. They are the opposites of other peoples. They are united, disciplined and hardworking. Such is their secret of prodigious and dizzying progress. It is because of this that they are the best and strongest in everything in the world. Their leaders are always well inspired and lead their people to Heaven. They don't deceive or betray their people. They are sincere, fair, visionary and responsible. They and their people are characterized by righteousness, patriotism and pragmatic voluntarism. They say loud and clear what they think and courageously do what they say. They love truth, justice, freedom, discipline, peace and well done job. It makes them happy.

Indeed, honesty makes happy and prosperous a people who practices it. In a country where everyone is honest, everyone is free, safe, peaceful, quiet. And everything is working very well for the benefit of everyone. Everyone contributes to the development, enrichment and protection of the country through their effort, their rigor, their courage, their endurance, their combativeness and their patriotism. This is the opposite of Africa where everyone is dishonest, barbaric, cheater, thief, corrupt, liar. These are westernized, neo-colonized, alienated Africans in Africa. Traditionalist peasants or villagers are different. They are virtuous. In Africa, all political and administrative leaders misappropriate state property for their own benefit and ruin their countries. Thus the African countries are all decadent, impoverished, plundered and destroyed by their intellectual, political and administrative elites. They are all in chronic underdevelopment. They suffer from obscure despotism and the charter of imperialism. Their populations are in total misery, distress and desolation. It is the general, popular misfortune created by the elites. This is not the case in America. Here, the national wealth is honestly shared with the population thanks to a rational justice system (distributive justice). To each according to his merit, his work and his needs. Justice and honesty triumph in America, to everyone's great happiness. Africa must imitate America to be saved. It must stop practicing dishonesty, injustice, vices from the charter of imperialism and the colonial pact.

Africa must put an end to its politics of self-flagellation, self-predation, self-slavery, self-destruction (suicide). It must espouse ascetic morality. It must apply the African Charter on the Rights of Peoples and Citizens that it has given to itself. It is its moral and legal compass. It is good for its progress, its liberation, its emancipation, its self-determination, its happiness, its dignity and its salvation. It must also apply **Afrocratism** as its official, general, continental political philosophy. This is our work, our patriotic contribution. It is good and essential for its rebirth, its progress, its political, economic, social, cultural development. Afrocratism shows it the way of its reconstruction, its influence and its power. It is the doctrine or the ideology of its revolution.

8

CIVILITY

America knows how to educate and train its citizens. It instills in them moral, legal and religious values. Isn't its national motto: "in God we trust"? Thus it produces wise citizens, disciplined and obedient to the established order. It makes civilized men and women. This makes its security, social peace, national cohesion, harmony and stability. America teaches good citizenship to its citizens so that they are loyal to it. Thus every

American is faithful to his duties as a citizen. America can boast of having succeeded in its educational and civilizing mission. It has very good citizens. The American population is perfectly integrated into the national order. It is submissive. There is no place for the outcasts, the anarchists, the nihilists, the marginalized, the rebels, the revolutionaries, the iconoclasts in America. Americans are really civilized, polite, courteous, humane, virtuous. They are very dignified, gentle. They all have a sense and awareness of the importance of order, discipline, cleanliness, the common good. They have political, historical, civic, social, cultural, spiritual, moral awareness.

Americans clearly know where they are coming from, where they are going, where they are passing. They clearly know their national goals and objectives (ideals). They are aware of what is good, useful, just, true, beautiful, legitimate, legal. They willingly and scrupulously respect the ideals, values, standards and virtues that make up greatness, dignity, power and the beauty of their country. They passionately love their country. They are very proud of it. They are fervent patriots and nationalists. They cannot therefore sabotage order, sow chaos, create anarchy and disgrace. They know that to destroy their beautiful and powerful country is to commit suicide. For them, law is sacred. Law is expression of general will and aims for the common good. American laws are democratic, republican, rational, just, legitimate. Obeying laws is the supreme duty for anyone. That is the dearest duty for the American citizens. Law is a sacred instrument. Americans are good disciples of J.J. Rousseau. Indeed, they are convinced that obedience to the law is freedom and happiness. Law is harsh but it is law. Dura lex sed lex, said the ancient Romans. Law is good. It saves everyone and the country. It prevents the country from falling into decadence and deadly imbroglio. It is the national compass. It is the pledge of national peace, security, consensus, understanding, cohesion, harmony and solidarity. The Romans were right to say: "Pro patria, pro lege" (for the homeland, for the law). Because there can be no viable, secure homeland without law. The homeland is a political, administrative, social organization. It is a state. It is a bundle of legal rules which functions as the guarantor of the security, peace, stability, happiness, order and discipline of the country. Law is therefore vital and indispensable. It is the foundation of the existence of civil society and men. It conditions absolutly individual and collective life. It separates men from animals.

Beware of people from elsewhere who do not respect their own laws. This is the most serious flaw that still puts African peoples in danger. This creates disorder, violence, barbarism, injustice, arbitrariness everywhere in Africa. Thus civil wars, armed rebellions, coups d'Etat, violation of national constitutions. Everyone does whatever he wants with impunity. Everyone cheats, steals, lies, harms public order and the general interest. The whole country and its property belong exclusively to the strongest, the most powerful individuals. That is too bad for the weak. They are at the mercy of the strong. No mercy for the helpless. They have no rights. The strong have the right of life or death over them. They are taillable and workable at mercy. African countries are jungles. They are baskets of crabs. The strongest devour the weak. This is the result of the absence or non-compliance with the laws. So law has no effect on the life of Africans. Morals and religion have any effect on Africans as well. Everyone owes his happiness, security, tranquility, peace and salvation to his strength, power, ability to defend himself, to fight, to eliminate, to dominate, to submit, to keep others away, to defeat them. It is the war of all against all in the name of happiness and interest. Everyone is everyone's adversary and enemy. National wealth and property belong only to the executioners without moral scruple (monsters). If America is a paradise, Africa is hell. How can we turn this hell into paradise? As long as the system called obscure despotism in Africa remains, nothing good will be possible for Africans. The solution to this problem lies in the application of Afrocratism to Africa. Afrocratism is a philosophy and an ideology for the revolution, development and rebirth of Africa.

9

PATRIOTISM

Americans are good patriots. They practice exemplary patriotism. What is patriotism? It is the fervent and passionate love of an individual for his homeland. It is a very powerful feeling which firmly attaches a citizen to his country. This leads the citizen to want to sacrifice himself for his country. A patriot is ready to defend his homeland at all costs. He does not count what it costs him because for him, the fatherland is the supreme value.

It is the supreme good. Homeland is the land of his father (pater in Latin), that is to say the family property, the family home where one was born and where members of his family live. By representation and by extension, homeland is, today, the country where one was born. It is the nation of an individual. Nation comes from the verb to be born. Nationalism, as a feeling or behavior, approaches patriotism.

To fully understand the meaning of the word patriotism, let's take a few concrete examples from history. The Japanese suicide bombers who took fighter jets to crash into enemy warships in WWII are patriots. They were doing this in the name of the total love they have for their country and their emperor. It is their sacred duty. Thomas Sankara, ex President of Burkina Faso was a very fiery patriot. His slogan or national motto was: "Fatherland or death, we will win!". He gave his life for the conquest of real and total independence, for the development, prosperity and sovereignty of his homeland. He died assassinated by imperialism and French neo-colonialism (martyr). Mouamar Gadhafi, the

Supreme Leader of the Libyan Revolution, was a patriot. He died assassinated by Western imperialism. He wanted the complete decolonization, the liberation, the sovereignty, the dignity, the prosperity, the power, the greatness, the development of Africa (martyr). Patrice Lumumba also. Mahatma Gandi was a patriot. He was assassinated. He wanted independence, liberation, sovereignty, happiness and prosperity for India, his homeland (martyr). These are very emblematic figures of patriotism that history presents to us.

How does American patriotism manifest itself? All American Presidents are fervent patriots who set an example for their compatriots. They work for the greatness, peace, freedom, power, continual development, unlimited all-out progress of America. All Americans seek the endless radiance of their country. The War of Independence against England, the War of Secession or of Integration helped to create the most powerful, prosperous and wealthy nation in the world. Americans are working hard, tirelessly, night and day, to move America further and make it stronger, more beautiful, more prosperous, more powerful.

For example, the former President Donald Trump nationalized the Federal Reserve and restored monetary sovereignty to the United States. He cut funds at the WHO and took his country out of all the international organizations that cost America a lot of money. He thus bailed out the state coffers. He canceled the Chinese 5 G. His slogan was to make America even bigger, more powerful, richer. His intention was to make America more beautiful and better. He kept blaming, denouncing, criticizing the Presidents of other countries. He gave them political, moral, civic, humanistic and patriotic lessons from his own example. He did not become President of the United States of America by force, injustice, dishonesty, war, coup d'Etat, armed rebellion, nor to enrich himself by stealing America's property and money. He did not change the American constitution in order to keep power manu militari, to stay in power for ever. He did not starve or impoverish Americans. On the contrary, he gave them work. He reduced the unemployment rate. He made American people happy. He gave them peace, security, serenity. He did not make war on the Americans or on the other peoples in the world. He preserved the moral and spiritual greatness of America (in God we trust). He reconciled America with its external enemies (North Korea). Africa needs Patriotic Presidents like American Presidents to be saved. President Donald Trump said: "The worst thing in Africa is that if you try to talk about what is right, they will beat you, imprison you or make you disappear". "Tell the truth, they will beat you up, imprison you or even make you disappear." He said again: "You all know that Blacks do not know how to govern themselves. Give them weapons and they kill each other". He also says: "If after 50 years of independence, you have not built the necessary infrastructure for your people, are you human beings?". He adds: "If you sit on gold, diamonds, oil, manganese, uranium... and your people have no food, are you humans?" Again, he adds: "If your only social project is to remain in power for life, are you human?" Again: "If you despise and shoot your own citizens like games, who will respect them?" These are patriotic lessons from the 45th US President to African Presidents.

EQUALITY

Equality of condition for all citizens is the sacred principle of modern political systems. It is the basis of state, republic, democracy. This is called equality of rights. It is the principle chosen, adopted and practiced by modern countries as something vital and absolute value. This means that in effect, all citizens of every country are equal before the law, that no one can be considered (or consider himself) superior to others. This principle must be reflected in daily political life. In other words, and in plain language, the justice of a country must treat all citizens in the same way. Equal fault, equal punishment. To each according to his work and his needs. Equal pay for equal work. To each citizen according to his merit (distributive justice). It is said that all men are born free, equal in rights and dignity (Universal Declaration of Human and Citizen Rights). This international law is more or less respected or applied by the nations of this world.

In Africa, for example, it is not respected by neocolonial states, corrupt, dishonest, unjust, barbarians, cynics, criminals, predators. In Europe, this law is respected by responsible, fair governments. In Asia, Buddhist, Confucianist, Hinduist and Taoist humanism and morals rule everyone. In America, Christian morals and humanism impose this law of equality and justice on all (in God we trust). Equality of condition is evident in everyday life. It's a reality. Equality in rights and dignity of all men is lived with rigor. It is sacred. This is applied to everyone. To each according to his actions, his merits, his work, his talents. All people are truly equal and responsible before the law. Equality is both theorized and practiced. It stems from moral, legal, religious doctrines and materializes in everyday American reality. Everyone's rights are strictly respected and guaranteed. There is no discrimination anywhere based on race, religion, social rank, wealth. There is no injustice or arbitrariness in the application of law. Any act which resembles discrimination is combated. The public slogan reads: if you see anything wrong, dangerous, report it to the police. "If you see something, say something". This is broadcast through loudspeakers in buses, subways. It's written and posted with a police phone number to use. Surveillance cameras are placed at strategic locations. They report all abnormal and illegal acts (tickets, misdemeanors and crimes) as eyewitnesses. We are everywhere watched, disciplined. Everyone is brought to heel. There is no room for disorder, filth, insecurity, violence and evil.

This is the big difference between America and the rest of the world, especially French-speaking Africa. In this part of the world, it is total laissez-faire and laissez-passer. It is the total absence of equality, cleanliness, discipline and justice. There are strong and weak, masters and slaves, executioners and victims, dominators and dominated, oppressors and oppressed. Inequality of condition is the principle that governs Africa. This is the regulatory standard, the general rule. Only the strong, the bandits, the powerful and the masters have rights. They have all the rights. There are no rights for the poor, the weak, the dominated, the unhappy, the needy. A villager, an illiterate and a peasant are sub-men in Africa. The latter are not counted in national life. They have no right or no dignity in front of the intellectual elites, intellecto-crats, modernists, occidentalocentrists who absolutely rule the country as ruthless slave traders and predator-oppressors. These bour-geois are the faithful servants of the execution-ers of slavery and Western colonialists. Their role is to keep the weak in bondage, suffering, misery and absolute helplessness eternally and to deliver all goods and riches to Western colonizers for crumbs which they receive for themselves as rewards. They are executioners.

They have the right of life or death over the weak. They have no accountability to their victims for the administration of the country or for their management of national property and wealth. They are not responsible to their victim-slaves. They are so only in front of their masters, employers. This system has been called **obscure despotism** by Edem Kodjo and **intellectocracy** by us. In order to fully understand these two concepts, one must read two books: **And Tomorrow Africa** (Edem Kodjo) and **Afrocratism against the New World Order** (François Adja Assemien).

JUSTICE

Justice is above all a vision of life. It's an idea, an ideal that shows men how to live together. As such, it regulates the whole society as a rule. It is an instrument created by thinkers, moralists, theologians, philosophers (Plato, in **La République**). This intellectual instrument defines order, morality (Kant), the functioning of society, of human life in society (Aristotle in **La Politique**). The idea of justice inspired the creation of societal, social, political and economic institutions. From its state of idea, vision, ideal as philosophy, ethics, morals, it has passed into concrete reality in the form of law, rule, standard of measurement of human behavior and actions. As a collective, conventional and regulatory norm, the ideal of justice makes it possible to judge, evaluate, reward or punish citizens. It defines what is just, good, acceptable, permitted, normal, legitimate, prohibited, abnormal, illegitimate, illegal (evil, misdemeanors, crimes). René Descartes said: "Correctness in thought, justice in actions". Justice levels men, puts them on an equal footing. All citizens of a country are equal and responsible under legal, moral (Kant) and religious law. Equal fault, equal punishment. Equal pay for equal work. All work merits salary. To each according to his merit, his work, his situation, his talents and his needs. The idea of justice is plural. It is subjective and relative. It varies between people and societies. Everyone has his idea or ideal of justice. Each people has its conception or definition of justice. This is what explains the difference between men, peoples, nations. This explains their ways of living, their social, economic, political, cultural, spiritual systems.

Generally, justice is distributive. It is on a pro rata basis. Justice puts men in competition. We take into account here the profitability, competence, productivity, creativity, intrinsic value, usefulness of each. We thus create a world of champions, elites, geniuses. It advances a country, develops a nation. Thus distributive justice created American gigantism and paradise. This form of justice allows America to dominate the world, to shine as the country that abounds in the most values and talents on earth. This is true in all areas of activity. It shows in art, in sport, in science, in technology, in literature. Justice reigns over Americans's life today. Americans are fair. They are not cheaters, corrupters, corrupt, dishonest. They know how to appreciate the talents, merits, values and skills of men. It is one of the causes of America's exceptional power, greatness, prosperity, progress and beauty. Africa has not understood that. Not at all. It remains unfair to itself. It cultivates injustice. It lives by and in injustice. That makes its smallness, its misery, its poverty, its ugliness, its helplessness, its infinite weakness and unworthiness. What a shame! An entire continent is languishing miserably in this deadly moral disease. Thus we will give centuries or millennia to Africa to develop, prosper and it will always remain in its present lamentable and shameful state or even regress. The same causes always generate the same effects. Negative behavior compromises future. Africa refrains from progress. It does not question itself. It does not do itself-criticism. It refuses freedom, revolution, rebirth, happiness, salvation, truth, justice. It locks itself in imbecility, stupidity, obscure despotism, self-destruction. It refuses to change, to be reasonable and rational. It refuses power, the struggle for its good, happiness, prosperity, success. It acts for its decadence, ruin, annihilation, end.

So **Africa is Africa's enemy.** Africa is Africa's worst deadly enemy. Africans are the executioners of Africans. They are sharks. They kill and devour each other. They are like crabs locked in a basket. Each African is a wolf for other Africans. Look, for example, at how they think, live, act politically. Watch how their Presidents become Presidents, how they govern their countries and how they lose power. It is very shameful. It hurts. It is pitiful. It is an infernal cycle of predation, coups d'Etat, armed rebellions, civil wars etc. It is barbarocracy, kleptocracy, mythocracy, bellocracy, autocracy… So goes Africa.

FREEDOM

Freedom is a reality for Americans. It is a fundamental value in America. Americans enjoyed it daily in their life. What is freedom? In sociological and political sense, freedom is the right or the power given to man to act or not to act within the framework of law. So whoever violates the law in force in a country will not be free. He will be deprived of his liberty. This means that he will be worried, punished, imprisoned or killed. It all depends on the degree, the seriousness of his fault (misdemeanor, contravention, crime). The culprit is not free in America. Whoever does things prohibited by law has no right to tranquility, security, peace, dignity and happiness. Whoever goes against righteousness, virtue, wisdom is deprived of his freedom. This is legitimate and fair.

Freedom is made up of several fundamental rights: right to life, right to good health, right to work, right to expression, right to movement, right to private enterprise, right to private property, right to marriage, right to association, right to education, right to vote etc. Freedom is not the absence of all constraints nor the power to do whatever you want. Because all that we want is not necessarily legal, legitimate, moral, virtuous, just. There are immoral, illegal, inhuman desires that are harmful to others. So to define freedom as libertinism, libertarianism, free will, sovereignty, that is dangerous. It is to fall into excess or the opposite of freedom as a moral and legal value. This amounts to deny the order established by society. It is to fall into anarchism, nihilism, egocentricity and solipsism. It is to fight social and civil peace, public security protected and guaranteed by law. It is to want to destroy happiness of all.

Freedom thus conceived cannot exist anywhere in the world. It is a utopia, a view of the mind, a metaphysical, theological illusion. It is opposed to historical reality. Indeed, the individual and the group always live within the framework of collective rules and conventional norms called laws which regulate the life of all and preserve the societal order. True freedom is a dynamic sum of collective constraints. It is a system of constraints and servitudes judiciously designed to maintain and consolidate order, safeguard civil society and secure human life, property and happiness. Absolute respect for the law by all is the guarantor of living together and everyone's happiness. Every reasonable and intelligent man should readily choose relative, conventional and conditional freedom. He must fight against utopian (simple dream) and dangerous freedom.

American freedom consists in respect for collective authority and discipline. Man was born free and everywhere he is free in civil society. Civil society with its constraints and wise laws make man free. "Obedience to the law that we have prescribed for ourselves is freedom," said J.-J. Rousseau (**Du Contrat social**). In other words, the individual frees himself by his conformity to the established order and to national or public discipline. The American republican and democratic state is the instrument which regulates and organizes the area of freedom for each and everyone. It has put all the salutary and necessary institutions in place. Every American respects them, maintains them and makes them work. He is the beneficiary, the profiteer. He carries order, law and discipline within him. He lives them in his mind, in his environment and in his daily life. He is opposed to the African. Indeed, the African is fundamentally anarchist, undisciplined. He lives in the greatest disorder and physical and moral filth. He despises and denies legal, moral and religious law. Every African is a wolf for the established order. He is an unrepentant destroyer of the state. He likes living in the stinking trash. He thinks that he will gain everything by doing this. That is his paradise, the place of his great happiness. Thus the former American President, Mr Donald Trump, could say that Africa is a dumping ground, a heap of garbage, a trash (shit hole), a place of shit. This is verified. Go, for example, to Ivory Coast (West/Africa) and you will see it. The Ivorian population is paradoxically struggling to keep Côte d'Ivoire in this horrible state. The current President of Ivory Coast, Mr Alassane Ouattara, meets the anger, opposition and fierce resistance of the Ivorian population in his political will to modernize, cleanse, beautify and develop Ivory Coast. He is told that he is a white man. He is told to leave the Ivory Coast which he wants to bring out in its pitiful and shameful state, as he found it, that is to say in the disorder, the dirt, the trash. The Dioula population (he himself is Dioula however) says that they prefer his predecessor, Mr Laurent Gbagbo. Because the latter left the Ivory Coast to its sad fate. He closed his eyes to disorder, filth, indiscipline, evil. For the Dioula, he was doing his job as President very well. He was doing their will. That enriched them. They say loud and clear: "Gbagbo kafissa". This means in Bambara linguage:

Gbagbo is better than Alassane Ouattara. Gbagbo is more useful, more interesting. Dioula women even wore uniform loincloths and marched against President Alassane Ouattara. On these loincloths, it was written: "Gbagbo kafissa". It is the phrase of protest, of popular anti-Alassane Ouattara insurrection. This means that the Ivorian disease is very serious, that the Ivorian wound is very deep. It is very shameful. It is very pitiful. It hurts. This anti-Alassane Ouattara or anti-development sling can be explained by a sort of collective Dioula superstition. According to this superstition, disorder, filth or uncleanliness (indiscipline, incivism) brings in money. In other words, cleanliness, discipline, order and beauty impoverish people or prevent them from making money. The term Dioula means trader. It is a generic term. The Dioula are the different peoples from the north of Côte d'Ivoire, Mali, Burkina Faso, Guinea Conakry, Senegal... whose main activity is trade. We see them settling everywhere, in disorder, near garbage cans, stinking dumps invaded by flies to sell all kinds of goods. Women and men transform gutters and sewers into shops. They settle there to sell their goods. The President Alassane Ouattara leads a tough battle against that in the districts of Abidjan, the economic capital of Ivory Coast. Under the regimes of its predecessors, household waste was placed squarely on the roads and formed "mountains". We weren't picking them up. They blocked the roads and prevented vehicles from moving. This was seen in the middle of Cocody, the presidential and diplomatic quarter. It was the height of shame and misfortune. It was a disaster in terms of public hygiene and urban sanitation.

13

PEACE

Peace is a major concern of America. Uncle Sam's country struggles very hard to preserve social peace, civic peace and world peace. The presence of the UN on its soil proves that peace is very dear to it. It is in America that we settle all the great conflicts in the world. America defends, monitors peace in the world. It intervenes where it is necessary to promote peace on earth. As it deeply loves peace, it had to make war on itself (Civil

War). Who wants peace prepares for war. War is thus a fatality according to Gaston Bouthoul. It is just for whom it is necessary and holy are its weapons according to Nicolas Machiavelli. The sacred ideal for everyone is peace. War is its main instrument. It is a necessary step. If there were other more legitimate and effective means of achieving peace, they would have to be resorted to, without going to war in the world. Because the cost of war is too high. War must be avoided to spare human lives which are sacred and to avoid costly material damage. While waiting to find peaceful means absolutely effective in addressing all global conflicts peacefully, that humanity can only employ war to resolve its problems of peace. It is about the just, necessary, legitimate, pacifist war. Thus the dissuasive, preventive, educational, civilizing war. We wage war in the name of peace which is the supreme end or the very dear and sacred universal value.

The other nations in the world have not understood this dialectic of peace and war. Certain nations make war an end in itself and for itself. They reverse the order of

things. It is regrettable and stems from mad-
ness, ignorance, imbecility of men and peoples. It is, for example, the case of Africans.
They confuse war and peace, end and means.
Their politicians practice obscure despotism,
autocracy, barbarocracy, violentocracy, kleptocracy, bellocracy, mythocracy. In this per-
versity and this political dynamic, they take
state power through civil war. They exercise
it through warlike violence. They lose the
exercise of this power through civil war. It's
systemic. So African countries live perma-
nently in violence, barbarism, terror, war. It
follows misery, suffering, atrocious poverty
of their populations. Peace is therefore a very
scarce commodity in Africa. It is impossible.
Its conditions of possibility do not exist. Only
the causes of war exist. This is why we are
witnessing conflicts, violence and genocides
in Africa. Man is a wolf for man in Africa.
Rulers are mortal enemies of populations.

In Côte d'Ivoire, for example, all the
Presidents and their regimes have waged war
on the Ivorian population from 1960 to the
present day. Ivorian politics are tribal, nepo-
tist, selfish. That is anti-republican, anti-dem-

ocratic, anti-state. It does not respect any rule, any moral law. It royally ignores legality and legitimacy. It operates on the basis of the most total arbitrariness and the most monstrous cynicism. It is obscure despotism based on predation, slavery, neocolonialism, the charter of imperialism, the colonial pact (Françafrique). Ivorian politics is the field of application of the law of the strongest, the most powerful, the most wicked, the most cruel, the most selfish, the wildest and the most barbaric. President Félix Houphouët-Boigny waged war against the Bété, the Abbey and the Agny Sanwi. President Konan Bédié waged war on the Dioula, on the Muslims. President Laurent Gbagbo waged war on the Dioula, on Muslims, on foreigners. President Alassane Ouattara is waging war on the populations of the West, Center and South of Côte d'Ivoire. Peace is totally absent in Côte d'Ivoire. Côte d'Ivoire is still a country at war.

14

SECURITY

Is America a Safe Country? Yes. What is security in a country? A country is secure when it is not in danger, when it is sheltered from any risk, from any catastrophic misfortune likely to cause its decadence, its instability, its ruin, its death. Countries that experience very serious political, economic, social, cultural crises or recurrent natural disasters (earthquakes, floods, wars, coups d'Etat, armed rebellions) are not safe. They are rather in danger. For example, African countries are in total insecurity because they are struck by the worst misfortunes or catastrophes caused by themselves and by their imperialist torturers, slavers and colonialists. They are still at war, in suffering, in pain, in fire. They are in hell. Foreign barbarians take everything arbitrarily (theft, looting, predation) and massacre their populations with impunity (genocides, risk of future extermination). They are deprived of all comfort, all happiness, all freedom, all security, all peace, all dignity. They are characterized by chronic instability and anarchy, ravaged by misery, indiscipline, poverty, disease, ignorance, barbarism, foreign and local violence, disunity, lack of solidarity and mutual aid. They spend their lives in genocidal and fratricidal wars of seizure and retention of state power. This is called obscure despotism by Edem Kodjo (in **And tomorrow Africa**) and barbarocracy by François Adja Assemien (in **Afrocratism against the new world order**). It is the height of distress.

America is opposed to African countries. It is the most secure country in the world. It has acquired all the necessary means in this regard. It has the most efficient and sophis-ticated means for its personal safety and global security. Americans live and sleep in peace. They are in joy, mirth, tranquility and happiness. This is the general situation. The rest depends on the psychological nature of each person. Each has his own character and temperament. Men do not have the same feelings in front of the same realities of this world. They don't all react the same way. So their judgments are subjective and relative. Psychologists say: "I see the world as I am and not as it is". There is no objectivity at the level of feelings, sensation and percep-tion. In truth, all the necessary structures, infrastructures and institutions exist and function wonderfully to bring the maximum well-being and happiness to all Americans. Every American gives his best at work. Who better better. And at all levels, people are very competent, rigorous, demanding, honest, responsible. Kindness, gentleness, compas-sion, politeness, courtesy, civility and selfless-ness absolutely reign in America. These are qualities and values that are very evident in America. Thus every American is very well protected, defended, supported and secured. In the event of danger or difficulty, everyone mobilizes, reacts promptly, spontaneously, effectively to rescue, help and save the victim.

Insecurity, injustice, disorder and indiscipline have no place in America. They have no right of citizenship there. If first I am a victim of injustice or violence, if my personal rights are violated, trampled upon by someone, I will benefit from free help and assistance from the police (911), the justice system, a volunteer lawyer. The police are omnipresent and omnipotent. Just call their number 911 and now they are at the scene of the reported event. They very quickly solve your problems of danger, accident, aggression, health, injustice, insecurity, violence. No one is above the law. All citizens are equal in rights and dignity. All are also free. It is the opposite of what is happening in other countries that we know, especially in Africa. In African countries, injustice, arbitrariness, corruption, barbarism, bloodthirsty dictatorship, state terrorism and other vices prevail. Evil is king everywhere. It is omnipresent in general administration, in political life, in socio-economic life, etc. There is real national competition in evil. The wicked are kings. They are admired, praised, glorified, rewarded, envied, blessed and imitated. They are a school in the country, at all levels, in all fields. A real national championship of evil is being played out. Honest, civilized, virtuous people are persecuted and punished (outcasts). They are without any merit. Rather, they are seen as bad examples, bad citizens. Evil is erected into a system of government. It is legal and legitimate. The good is a vice, a defect, a gross fault, a misdemeanor, a crime. Good is prohibited and punished.

In America, on the contrary, thugs of all stripes are tracked down, wherever they can be found, to their last entrenchments. Surveillance cameras monitor everything. Any violation of the law found is punished. There is no complacency, laxity, corruption, nepotism, negligence, tolerance possible at this level. Your life and your goods are absolutely yours. They are strictly observed by all. The forces of order and security really exist and function effectively and efficiently. They fulfill their missions perfectly without cheating or betrayal. They are loyal and faithful to their duties and their forward-looking responsibilities. They do not lack competence or zeal in their work. They are hyper-equipped with technical and professional resources. Each police officer has a well-equipped service vehicle. Americans are fair, sincere, honest, caring, reasonable, friendly, supportive, kind, helpful, sympathetic, sociable. Africans will gain everything by imitating them.

15

STABILITY

Is America a stable country? Yes, very stable. It is a country which is sheltered from all destabilizing and destructive violence such as coups d'Etat, civil wars, armed rebellions and bloody revolutions. What generally causes the instability of a country is injustice, frustration, disorder, bad economic and social situations and political crises resulting from the mode of seizure of power and government. But America is not a banana republic nor a despotic nation like the African countries which are characterized by obscure despotism and barbarism. The American political system is rational, legitimate and salutary. It is not disputed by the population. It is not an autocratic, mythocratic, kleptocratic, individualized or diffuse system. Rather, it is a legal and institutionalized power. This type of power ensures the legal equality of all, safeguards the freedom of each. This political system is government of the people by the people and for the people according to Abraham Lincoln, ex-President of the United States. Here, the rulers and the ruled are identical. It is **democracy.**

In theory, all political regimes have the same ends. It is a question of ensuring the legal equality of all, of safeguarding the freedom of each citizen. But, in fact, equality is compromised in regimes where government is in the hands of one (monarchy) or in the hands of a few (oligarchy). And freedom seems unevenly distributed between regimes. If it is true, as Hegel teaches, that in a monarchy only one is free, that in the aristocracy many are free, well in democracy everyone is free. The goal of democracy is individual freedom posted as the end. The state is the necessary means for the achievement of individual happiness, security and freedom. It is a set of disciplinary rules to promote collective life. Democratic politics has an instrumental value or function. Because it consists in determining fair, rational, egalitarian laws, capable of harmonizing, balancing particular interests and creating the common good or general interest. It is a social contract or a free convention according to J.-J. Rousseau.

This is not yet a dream or a reality for most countries in the world. Especially in Africa neocolonized by the West, the peoples are very far from thinking of democracy (ignorance, obscurantism) and wanting to achieve it. African intellectuals and political elites practice egoistic, egocentric, colonialist, predatory, criminal intellectocracy. It is a despotic, autocratic system based on the slaughter of the popular masses (genocide), barbarism (barbarocracy), war (bellocracy), ethnism (ethnocracy), tribalism (tribalocracy). Power is seized by force, violence, cruelty (coup d'Etat, armed rebellion, civil war). We reign by force, cruelty, barbarism, wickedness, cynicism, selfishness, nepotism, corruption, theft, predation, sadism, demagoguery, lies... Such a system is the opposite of republican, democratic, moral, humanist, virtuous, salutary politics. This even excludes the notion of state. It is a denial of state and of politics. It is monstrous and diabolical. It is a slave system based on Colbert's Black Code, on the Charter of Imperialism and on the Colonial Pact imposed on Africans by the very dangerous General de Gaulle (cynicism). It is a mafia, imperialist, terrorist system which distances the African peoples from any idea and any desire for political, economic, financial, monetary independence, freedom-liberation, autonomy, self-determination, sovereignty, development, dignity, peace, happiness, power, prosperity, struggle for life and salvation.

SOLIDARITY

Solidarity is a virtue, a value very important to Americans. It is practiced everywhere, among the American population. It reflects a relationship of interdependence, mutual assistance and mutual aid. Solidarity is a moral, humanist and religious law. It is expressed through compassion, love of neighbor, empathy, brotherhood, friendship, generosity, charity, altruism, helpfulness. This is based on humanism, civility and ascetic morals which are the manifestations of conscience and Reason. It takes place when the individual understands that he is responsible for everyone and that everyone is responsible for him. It is the law of reciprocity of duty. Americans are aware of being responsible for each other (moral and civic duty). This reflects the awareness by all of the universal fraternity and friendship which unites men in the community, in the human or national family. From there, everyone works, acts for the good health, success, security, well-being, freedom of all. Thus the misfortune of an individual is experienced collectively as the misfortune of all.

Everyone willingly sacrifices himself to make life pleasant, easy and beautiful for everyone. Thus social services abound and function wonderfully. They are very zealous, dynamic, efficient and beneficial. Many people willingly work as volunteers in various social, humanitarian and charitable activities. For example, firefighters, humanitarian workers, reception centers dealing with the well-being and plight of foreigners, refugees, immigrants, the poor, the destitute, the ministries of social affairs and public health, CASA de Maryland etc. America is therefore making one of the boldest socialism on earth. It is perhaps even more socialist than countries which claim to be socialists. It makes humanist and humanitarian socialism very salutary. Americans are neither individualistic nor selfish. They believe in God (in God we trust) and therefore they think they are children of God. They are all brothers to each other as sons of God. So they are required to do each other good and nothing but good. It is their religious and moral duty. Selflessness or charity is a divine law, a heavenly command. It is an absolute imperative for Americans. To believe in God is to love your neighbor as yourself. God is love. This is why believing Americans are good, charitable, and supportive of one another. America is living its religious faith. It is practicing its creed in truth.

Here again, America is exemplary. It constitutes a model to be emulated by other countries. America is a school for African countries which are sinking mortally into division, conflict, fratricidal, genocidal, senseless, stupid wars. Africans are totally lacking in saving solidarity. They only betray each other, harm each other and kill each other by selfishness, greed, wickedness, jealousy, hatred. They do not understand that solidarity constitutes a saving weapon, a privileged instrument of their liberation, their development, their prosperity, their greatness, their power, their happiness and their dignity in the face of their enemies. They do not understand that union, solidarity and will give victory in the face of adversity. Together and in fraternal union, the termites succeed in building their termite mound, which is a very complex and admirable castle. Together and united, English Pilgrims and Puritans built the most beautiful and powerful nation in the world known as the United States of America. Africans need to ponder and understand these illuminating examples that can open the eyes of the blind and one-eyed.

DISCIPLINE

Discipline is a teaching intended to make good citizens. It aims to make citizens civilized and human. It is inculcated in a people to make them wise, virtuous. It is made up of morals, law, religion and good citizenshif. Americans have received this teaching. They are disciplined. It does America a lot of good. This was made possible through education, coercion or police repression. The fear of the police officer is said to be the beginning of wisdom. That is true. Everyone is brought to heel in America. Indeed, the police are not kidding in America. They don't play. They are not complacent, irresponsible, corrupt, corruptible, light-hearted. They are rather rigorous, very serious, competent, worthy. They do their job very well. As agents of public order and security, they watch and control the country and people with vigilance. They are present wherever it is useful and necessary. This deters thugs, delinquents and criminals. This prevents them from acting with impunity and taunting the population. The police keep everyone at bay. If you make a mistake, if you break the law, you will be called to order. You will be corrected, rectified by justice. "Dura lex sed lex" (hard law but law), said the ancient Romans in Latin.

Discipline made America strong, powerful, beautiful, clean, prosperous, rich, and ruler of the world. Thanks to the respect for morals, religion and law by all and to the maintenance of public order, America is the most powerful, the most beautiful and the greatest country in the world. It is at peace, admired and envied. The assets of its success are the three elements or values of the Ivorian national motto: Union, Discipline, Work. The United States of America is a united, disciplined and hardworking country. And the Ivory Coast, which officially wears these fine values on its forehead, is not united, disciplined and hardworking. It does not do any good with these values. It's a waste. Ah, poor Africa! Côte d'Ivoire is underdeveloped. It is a poor and indebted country. Its populations (60 ethnic groups) are divided, disunited, undisciplined, lazy, corrupt, unworthy and enslaved by neo-colonialist France.

When will Africa wake up and start fighting for union, discipline, labor, emergence, development, independence, liberation, sovereignty, peace, security, dignity and power? Strongly that this be done quickly for the great happiness of Africans! There's no point in wearing a label or owning a glorious motto that you can't live up to. It's scandalous. It is shameful. It is unworthy. It is irresponsible. A national motto must serve as a compass, as a strong and regulating idea for saving and glorious actions. Too bad that in Africa the national mottos are not respected, lived, translated into facts, in the behavior of citizens. This is a public, official, national scam. It is political swindle (demagoguery). And that does not shock anyone in these African countries. We do not see any problem. Everyone finds this normal (general complicity in evil). Everyone is in bad faith. Everyone is dishonest (collective suicide, collective irresponsibility). All Africans are silent on this subject. Nothing matters to Africans. There is no embarrassment or shame for Africans. Feelings of modesty, dignity, shame, pride, do not reside in anyone. So everything is allowed in Africa. Evil is permitted there. No one has a noble vision or a virtuous ideal, salutary for his country in Africa. It is even forbidden to dream, to want to transform Africa into an earthly paradise. Rather, we should leave Africa in the trash where it is. Should we then despair of Africa? Geniuses, sages, heroes, martyrs have no value in Africa. They are without any merit. They are fought, persecuted to death. This is how Africa works. So Africa is the kingdom of paradoxes and antagonistic contradictions.

HAPPINESS

What is happiness? Is it the best shared thing in America? Generally, we oppose happiness to unhappiness. Thus happiness would be the absence of unhappiness, that is to say of suffering, of danger. For example, a sick person is not happy. A poor man is not happy. A slave is not happy. A prisoner is not happy. A colonized person is not happy. He who is hungry or thirsty is not happy. The one who is frustrated, deprived of all his fundamental rights is not happy. But he who is in joy, mirth, pleasure is happy. Thus defined, happiness can be granted to some and denied to others. The situations and conditions described are ephemeral, accidental. Happiness thus appears contingent. This means that if we define happiness only in relation to these transient, fleeting things (physical, psychological, sociological, political, economic, historical), we remain in ignorance, error, delusion. We are mistaken about the true, noble and profound nature of happiness.

The wise see happiness differently. They get to the bottom of it and find that happiness is not something mundane, superficial, material like a gift one receives from someone, which can be snatched, taken away, deleted. For them, happiness is a lasting state of mind, the fruit of hard and personal work on oneself. It is obtained through self-discipline, the cultivation of moral, ascetic virtue. It presents itself as a very pure state of mind, freed from all toxic feelings, all emotions, all toxic passion, pacified and stable. It is inner balance, harmony and serenity. The

Stoics and Epicureans call it ataraxia. That is peace of soul, of spirit. It is the fact of being in perfect harmony with oneself, with others (nature, universe, world). Happiness is the state of satisfaction of body and mind. It is the state of fullness of man. A person who has met both the demands or needs of his body and his mind can be said to be happy. The needs of the body are material goods and pleasures. For example, eating, drinking, making love, sleeping, dressing... (natural and necessary needs). The needs of the spirit are knowledge, truth, ascetic virtue. Happiness excludes ignorance, delusion, falsehood, error, dishonesty, lies, wickedness, vices. It excludes the lack. The man who lacks food for his body and his mind is unhappy. He is opposed to happiness.

Americans know that very well. And they avoid misery, destitution and moral and physical poverty. They have given themselves the means that allow them to be in healthy balance and harmony. So they properly maintain their body and mind. They are well educated, well cultured. They have the essential knowledge (science, philosophy, morals, ethics, technology). They have the knowledge, the manners and the know-how. Their minds and bodies are well nourished and satisfied. More than any other people on earth, they have developed their economy to the highest level. They are the richest and most prosperous on earth. Their social and economic system is at the top level. It is very efficient and beneficial. Americans produce all consumer goods and things. They are in overabundance. No other people on earth have done as much as they have. They are exceptional, unparalleled creative geniuses. They do everything brilliantly. They are particularly brave, courageous, inventive, hardworking. Their golden rule is the culture of excellence. Excellence in all areas and in the detail of everyday life. Laziness, mediocrity, weakness have no place in America. Their place is elsewhere, especially in Africa. This is why today's Africans are the last on earth, in this world of deadly competition.

CONCLUSION

America is a paradise and elsewhere it is hell (especially Africa). Americans have given themselves the maximum happiness thanks to their will to power, their merits, their creative genius, their infinite talents. They have built a gigantic civilization that challenges the whole world and dominates the whole earth. This is very impressive and beneficial. The American people are so smart and so wise. They understood that union, discipline and work make kings and gods on earth. So they cultivated and developed these beneficent and saving values thoroughly, ad infinitum. They derive colossal benefits from it. They are very happy. They are very proud of themselves. They are right. They are very deserving. It is to their honor and glory. They are to be congratulated and imitated. They are the model, the exemplary. America must serve as a school for the whole earth, for all the countries which vegetate and languish in misery. It must be the salutary school of Africa which causes so much shame and so much pity. Africa, however, has the key words that make America's infinite power and greatness, such as its slogans and its national motto: union, discipline, work. Unfortunately, it does nothing serious, good, useful, salutary about it. Rather, it does the opposite of the message of these key words. Pity! It's a deadly mess. It's scandalous. Africa is opposed to good. It cultivates evil. It refuses its happiness and the way to its salvation.

America lives in and by the Ivorian's motto which is a very powerful and regulating philosophy and ideology. What matters and saves the world is action, practice. National thought must be applied for the happiness of all. Union, discipline and work constitute the key and the secret of success, happiness, power, salvation, liberty, sovereignty, independence, autonomy, peace, security. They must not be empty words. They must serve as a support, a spring, an engine for the creation of paradise. The will for power, happiness, prosperity must animate and direct all peoples towards union, discipline and work. America has masterfully and heroically taken this glorious step. It succeeded admirably in this experiment. It clearly shows the rest of the world what needs to be done to achieve development, tremendous growth, greatness. It shows how to remove hell on earth and access heaven. The duty of the suffering, underdeveloped, counterdeveloped countries (African countries) is to understand this American lesson and to practice it from now on. How many times should we say this and repeat it to African countries, countries of scandals and paradoxes? Indeed, how can one choose or give oneself a salutary, glorious motto and contradict it by suicidal behavior of sheep and devil? How can you betray yourself in such a shameful and deadly way? Why do you choose the path to paradise and you head to hell? The demagoguery, bad faith and Machiavellianism of dishonest politicians can never develop or save a country. Wanting one thing and its opposite is a game of crazy people and devil. It is monstrous. This has catastrophic consequences. Unlike African countries which benefit infinitely from the bounties of nature and God, Asian countries are totally deprived of natural resources, mining, raw materials. But they are doing well. Why? Because they are wise, united, disciplined and hardworking. They are inventive, nationalist, brave. They take up their challenges. They are to be congratulated. It is now up to African countries to learn to respect and apply their slogans and their national motto which are very flattering and very attractive: democracy, republic, freedom, independence, equality, fraternity, unity, dignity, power, greatness, development, growth, progress, prosperity, justice, revolution, rebirth, sovereignty, self-determination, autonomy. All this is just window dressing. Africans, We must now move on to concrete actions. We must act, take it seriously and change Africa.

www.ingramcontent.com/pod-product-compliance
Lightning Source LLC
Chambersburg PA
CBHW071838190726
48292CB00005B/1822